FOREST FEELINGS

MASON THE MOOSE FEELS MAD

by Megan Atwood
illustrated by Carissa Harris

GRASSHOPPER

Tools for Parents & Teachers

Grasshopper Books enhance imagination and introduce the earliest readers to fiction with fun storylines and illustrations. The easy-to-read text supports early reading experiences with repetitive sentence patterns and sight words.

Before Reading

- Discuss the cover illustration. What do they see?
- Look at the picture glossary together. Discuss the words.

Read the Book

- Read the book to the child, or have him or her read independently.
- "Walk" through the book and look at the illustrations. Who is the main character? What is happening in the story?

After Reading

- Prompt the child to think more. Ask: Mason feels mad. How do we know? What does he say and do that show he is angry?

Grasshopper Books are published by Jump!
5357 Penn Avenue South
Minneapolis, MN 55419
www.jumplibrary.com

Library of Congress Cataloging-in-Publication Data

Names: Atwood, Megan, author.
Harris, Carissa, illustrator.
Title: Mason the moose feels mad / by Megan Atwood; illustrated by Carissa Harris.
Description: Minneapolis, MN: Jump!, Inc., 2024.
Series: Forest feelings | Includes index.
Audience: Ages 7–10.
Identifiers: LCCN 2023029039 (print)
LCCN 2023029040 (ebook)
ISBN 9798889969662 (hardcover)
ISBN 9798889969679 (paperback)
ISBN 9798889969686 (ebook)
Subjects: CYAC: Anger—Fiction. | Moose—Fiction.
Brothers—Fiction. | LCGFT: Animal fiction. | Picture books.
Classification: LCC PZ7.A8952 Mas 2024 (print)
LCC PZ7.A8952 (ebook)
DDC [E] —dc23
LC record available at https://lccn.loc.gov/2023029039
LC ebook record available at https://lccn.loc.gov/2023029040

Editor: Jenna Gleisner
Direction and Layout: Molly Ballanger
Illustrator: Carissa Harris

Printed in the United States of America at
Corporate Graphics in North Mankato, Minnesota.

Table of Contents

Learning to Let It Out

Mason the moose loves playing hide-and-seek. He is next to seek. He cannot wait for his turn!

His brother Marcus finds the last hider.

"Everyone hide! I'm seeking again," he calls. "One . . . two . . . three . . ."

"Hey! It was my turn!"
Mason yells.

"You're always too slow,
Mason. It's my turn now!"
Marcus laughs.

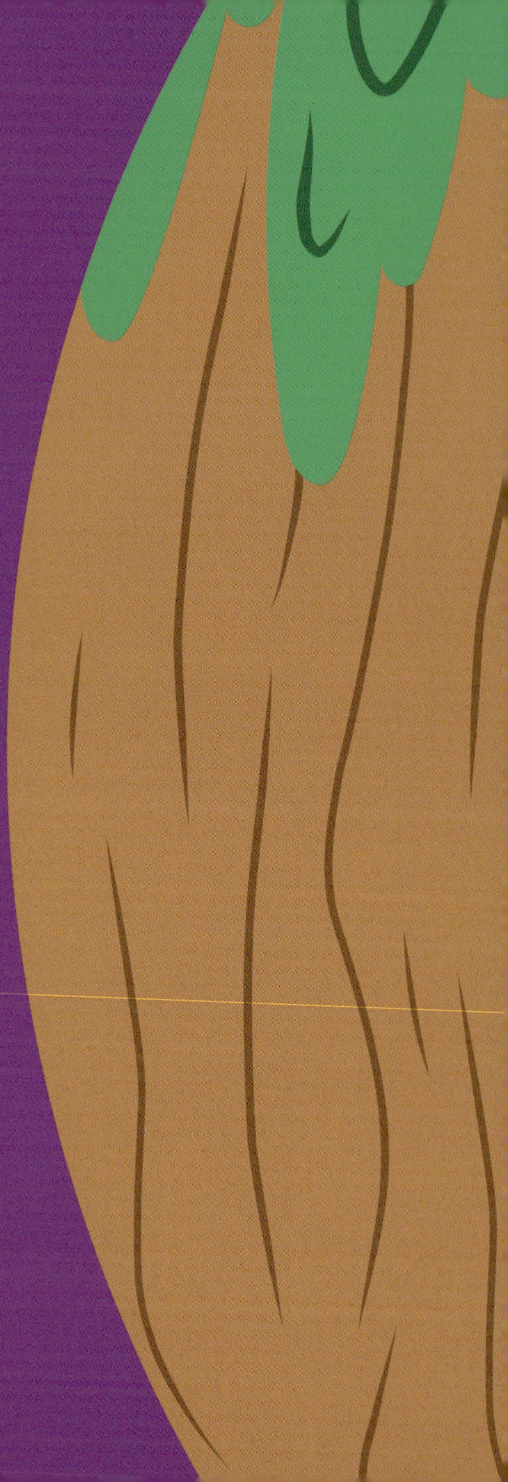

A hot feeling moves from Mason's hooves to his antlers. His jaw clenches. He feels his eyebrows furrow.

"Four . . . five . . . six . . ." Marcus counts.

Mason can't take it anymore.
He stomps his hooves and charges.
He rams his antlers into Marcus.

"What was that for?!" Marcus yells.

Mason yells back, "You stole my turn!"

The brothers lock antlers as they argue.

"Stop it before someone gets hurt!" Scout the squirrel says.

Mason storms off. He goes to his favorite clearing to cool down.

He feels like he needs to move. He runs as fast as he can.

Next, he rams into a tree.
He needs to let the mad out.

Then he swims. Calm feelings start to replace his angry feelings. Mason thinks about how he acted.

He walks back to his friends.

"I'm sorry I hurt you," he says to Marcus. "I was really mad. But I found better ways to let my anger out. I won't do it again."

"I forgive you," Marcus says. "I'm sorry, too. I shouldn't have taken your turn. Do you want to seek now?" he asks.

The brothers knock antlers before Mason goes to count. He feels much better after learning to let it out.

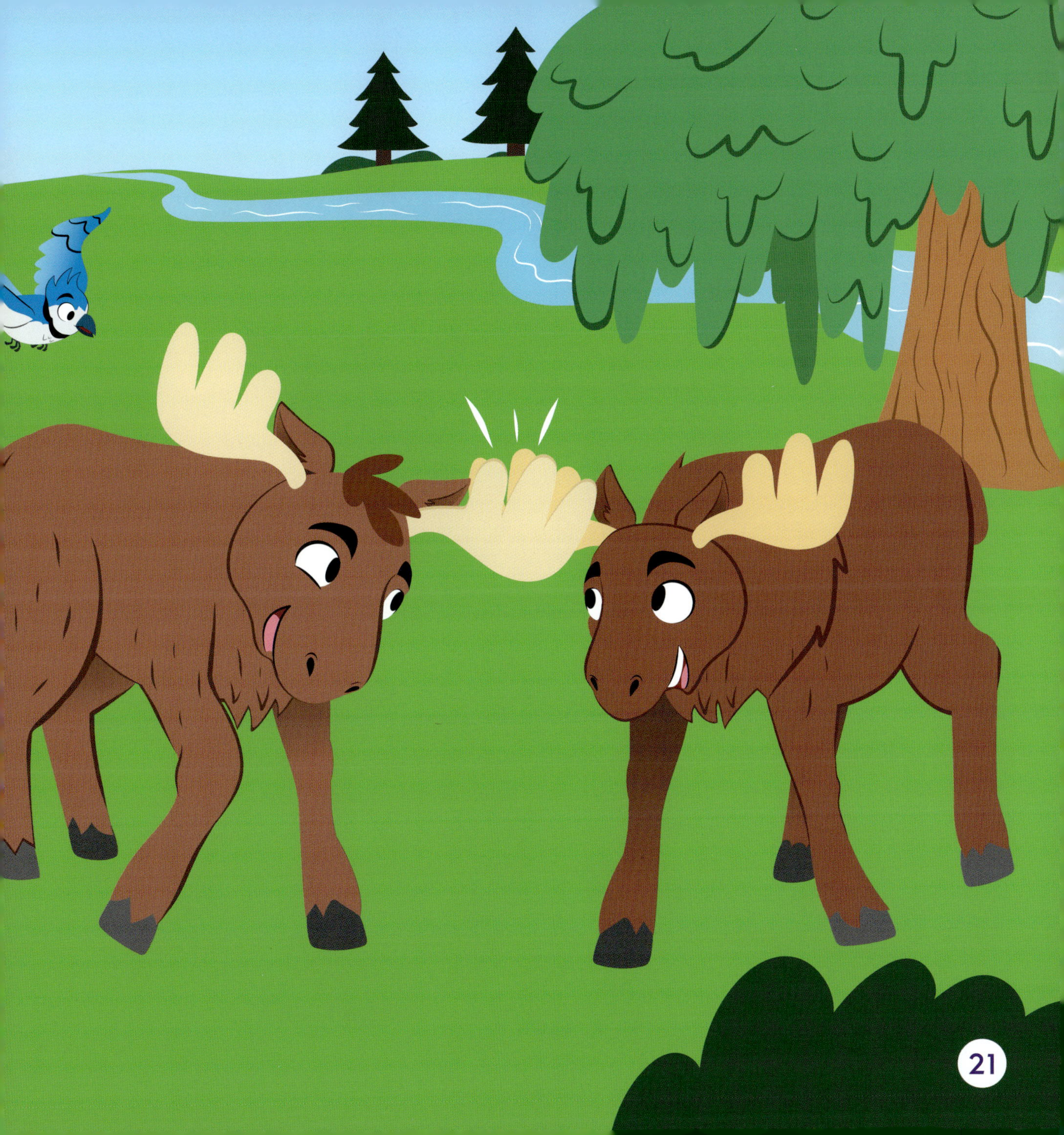

Let's Review!

Look at the scenes below. Point to those that show Mason mad. How do you know?

Picture Glossary

argue
To disagree when talking about something.

charges
Attacks in a rush.

clearing
An open area in a forest.

clenches
Closes tightly.

furrow
To wrinkle up.

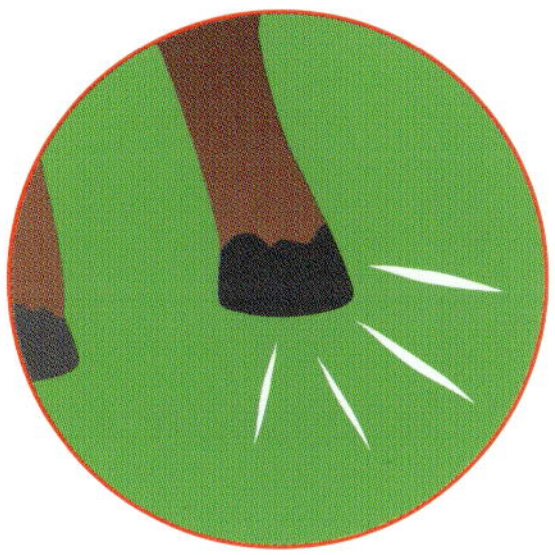

stomps
Bangs one's foot down in anger.

Index

To Learn More

Finding more information is as easy as 1, 2, 3.

1. Go to www.factsurfer.com
2. Enter "**Masonthemoosefeelsmad**" into the search box.
3. Choose your book to see a list of websites.